P9-DHT-332

THE GIANT OF SEVILLE

A "Tall" Tale Based on a True Story

DAN ANDREASEN

Abrams Books for Young Readers
New York

3 0076 00099 8363

Library of Congress Cataloging-in-Publication Data:
Andreasen, Dan.
The giant of Seville / by Dan Andreasen.
p. cm.
ISBN13: 978-0-8109-0988-5
ISBN10: 0-8109-0988-X
1. Bates, Martin Van Buren, b. 1845 2. Giants—
Ohio—Biography. I. Title.

GN69.22.B38A53 2006
599.9'49—dc22
[B]2006013579

Text and illustrations copyright
© 2007 Dan Andreasen
Photograph in Author's Note courtesy of
Don Gottlieb, Seville Historical Society

Book design by Chad W. Beckerman
Production Manager: Alexis Mentor

Published in 2007 by Abrams Books for Young
Readers, an imprint of Harry N. Abrams, Inc.

All rights reserved. No portion of this book may be
reproduced, stored in a retrieval system, or transmitted
in any form or by any means, mechanical, electronic,
photocopying, recording, or otherwise, without written
permission from the publisher.

Printed and bound in China
10 9 8 7 6 5 4 3 2 1

HNA
harry n. abrams, inc.
a subsidiary of La Martinière Groupe
115 West 18th Street
New York, NY 10011
www.hnabooks.com

TO MY SON, BRET
—D. A.

LIFE WAS TOO QUIET in the little town of Seville, Ohio. Some would say it was so quiet that if you listened carefully you could hear the corn grow. Nothing exciting ever happened.

But one day a stranger came to town on the noon train. He was so tall that the only way he could ride in the passenger car was to sit sideways on the seat with his head and shoulders sticking out of the window. This stranger was a giant.

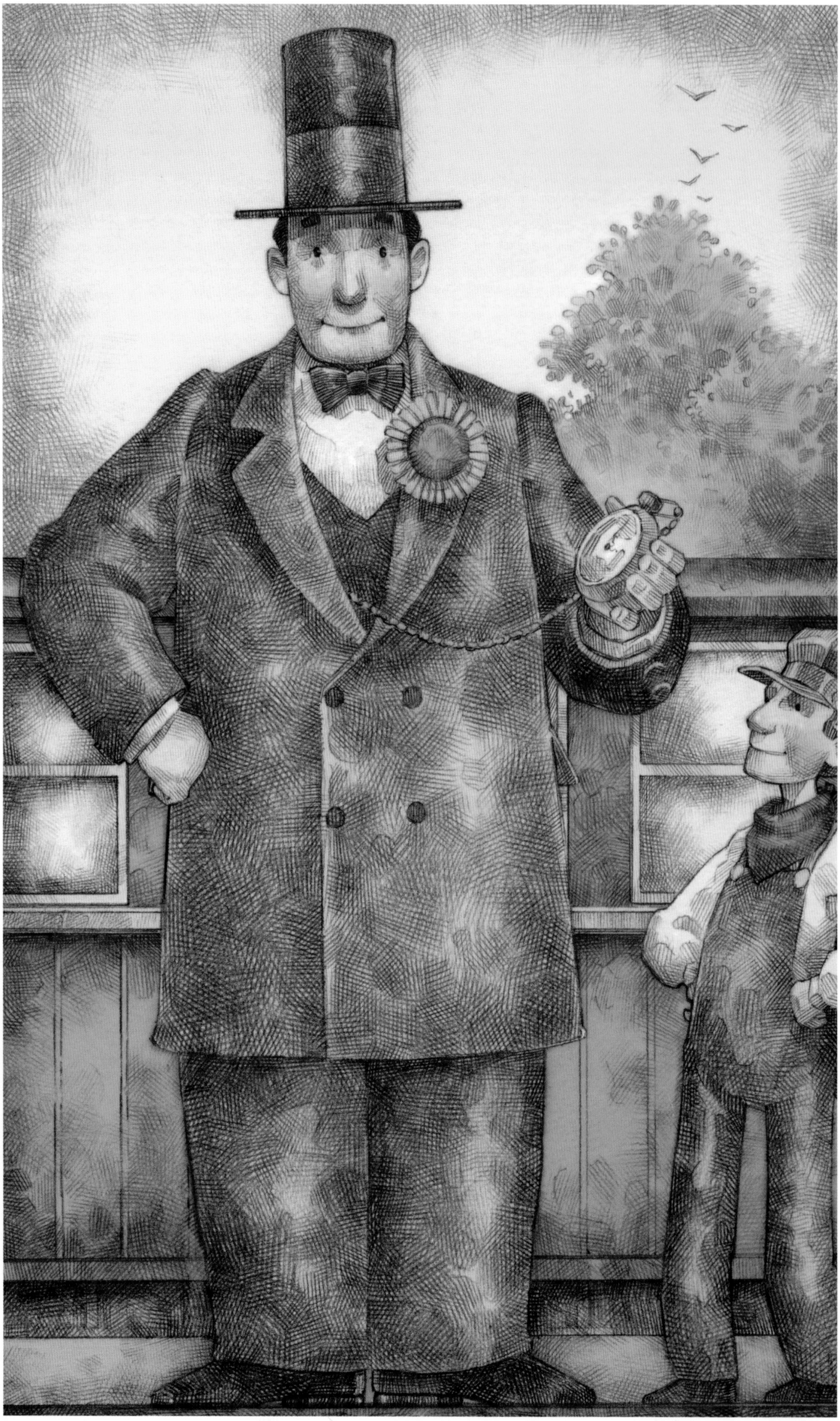

As the train slowly came to a stop at the station platform, the giant couldn't stand another minute in the cramped car, so he decided to climb out. With his hand on his back, he groaned, straightening to his full height.

He was dressed in a fine coat and vest, and perched atop his huge head he wore a stovepipe hat the size of a pickle barrel! At the end of a long gold chain he wore a pocket watch as big as a saucer. In his lapel was a bright yellow sunflower.

It took an hour for two porters to wrestle the giant's massive steamer trunk from the train. Stenciled on the side of the trunk in gold letters were the words CAPTAIN MARTIN VAN BUREN BATES EIGHTH WONDER OF THE WORLD.

As Captain Bates strode down Main Street with his trunk under his arm, word of his arrival traveled fast. Soon a crowd of people gathered to follow the giant through town.

Captain Bates went straight to old Mrs. Crawley's boardinghouse. The sign that hung beside the front door read, "All peaceable folk welcome." So the captain rang the bell.

Old Mrs. Crawley answered the door. Without even a whisper about the captain's amazing size, she calmly said, "What brings you to town?"

The stranger kindly replied, "I've traveled the world over in the circus with my wife, who is every inch my height. Together we've entertained royalty and common folk alike. But now we're tired of show business and just want to live a quiet life like everyone else. So I left my dear wife back east and boarded a train to search out the perfect place for our home. But it seems I'm just too big for every town I visit."

NOW THIS WAS the most exciting thing ever to happen to the sleepy town of Seville. All the townsfolk decided right then and there to make the giant feel right at home. Old Mrs. Crawley was a gracious hostess. She showed him to her finest room, the one with the king-size bed.

The bed may have suited a king, but later that night Captain Bates was uncomfortable. Quietly, he opened the window of his room and stretched his legs out to full length.

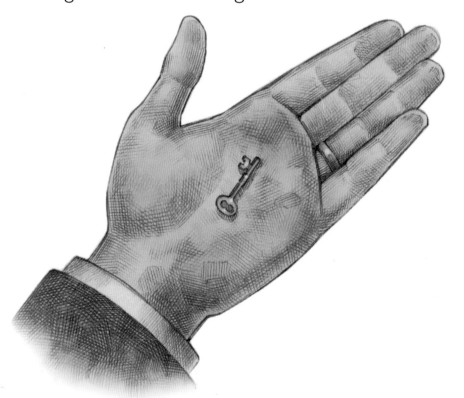

Old Mrs. Crawley, being very sensitive to drafts, soon discovered the captain's sleeping arrangements. "He'll catch his death of cold," she said. So she bundled up in her warmest robe, and with the help of several neighbors, she built a roaring bonfire just outside his window.

The next morning, Captain Bates awoke rested and refreshed, but poor old Mrs. Crawley was exhausted from tending the fire all night long.

Although she was very tired, Mrs. Crawley immediately set to work preparing breakfast for her special guest. But her griddle couldn't keep up with the captain's appetite for johnnycakes! So several of the town's ladies showed up to help old Mrs. Crawley. Together they mixed four gallons of cake batter and had five frying pans going at once.

After he had his fill, the captain leaned back in his chair with his hands on his belly and sighed. "Thank you kindly, ladies. That was the finest meal I've had in quite a spell!"

While sitting with the captain, Mrs. Crawley hit upon an idea. "We'll have a square dance tonight in the parlor!" She beamed. "This way you can meet all the townsfolk, and then I'm sure you'll decide that Seville is the perfect town for you and your wife."

That night, everyone in town turned out for the big dance. The furniture was pushed off to one side, and the carpet was rolled up. The sheriff of Seville sat at the piano, and the barber played the fiddle.

As the music and dancing increased to a fever pitch, all the guests cleared the floor and formed a large circle. In the center, Captain Bates danced a jig with such vigor that everything began to shake.

Suddenly, there was a loud crash! When the dust cleared, everyone noticed a large hole in the floor. The crowd peered down and saw that Captain Bates had fallen through! He sat in the cellar surrounded by splintered wood.

The men fetched a ladder to help the captain up. Luckily, the only thing injured was his pride. Captain Bates turned to old Mrs. Crawley and said, "I'm mighty embarrassed and sorry for all of the damage I've done, especially after you've been so nice to me. Please add the cost of repairs to my bill. Perhaps it's best I catch the train in the morning. I guess I'm too big for Seville after all."

BRIGHT AND EARLY the next morning, the men and women of Seville arrived. They were carrying hammers and saws and kegs of nails. The captain thought they had come to repair the damage to Mrs. Crawley's floor, but he was wrong. A bugle began to play, and everyone marched together toward the edge of town. Old Mrs. Crawley took the captain's hand, and they followed.

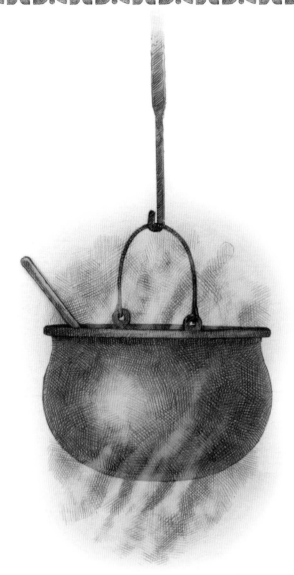

The women set up a big kettle and began preparing food as the men started to work laying foundation stones. The captain thought he was joining a barn-raising party, but he wasn't. The men were building a house. A giant-size house!

The captain was touched by the kindness of the people of Seville. And it was then that he realized he could not live in any other town.

Captain Bates sent a telegram to his wife to let her know he had found a town where the people were small but their hearts were giant.

A few days later, Anna Bates arrived. The whole town of Seville turned out to witness as Captain Bates carried his wife over the threshold of their new home. And the size was just right.

AUTHOR'S NOTE

Martin Van Buren Bates was born a baby of normal size on November 9, 1845. But he continued to grow until he was twenty-eight years old, reaching a height of seven feet eleven and a half inches and a weight of 525 pounds.

In 1861, at the start of the Civil War, Martin enlisted as a private in the Fifth Kentucky Infantry. He was promoted several times over the next few years, eventually achieving the rank of captain.

After the war, he joined the circus and was billed as "The World's Tallest Man." While touring with the circus in Halifax, Canada, he met Anna Swan. Anna Swan stood almost eight feet tall! She decided to join the circus with Martin, and together

Mrs. A. H. Bates,
Born August 6th, 1848.
Height 7 feet 11¼ inches.
Weight 413 Pounds.

Capt. M. V. Bates,
Born November 9th, 1845.
Height 7 feet 11¼ inches.
Weight 478 Pounds.

they toured throughout Europe. In 1871, they were married in London and Queen Victoria presented the newlyweds with a matching set of oversize diamond-studded gold watches. Martin and Anna became history's tallest known married couple.

After touring with the circus for many years, the couple settled down in Seville, Ohio, and built a house on one hundred thirty acres of farmland. The house was complete with fourteen-foot-high ceilings and eight-foot-high doors, and the furniture was built to order. Martin and Anna later returned to circus life, but they would forever be Seville's most famous residents.